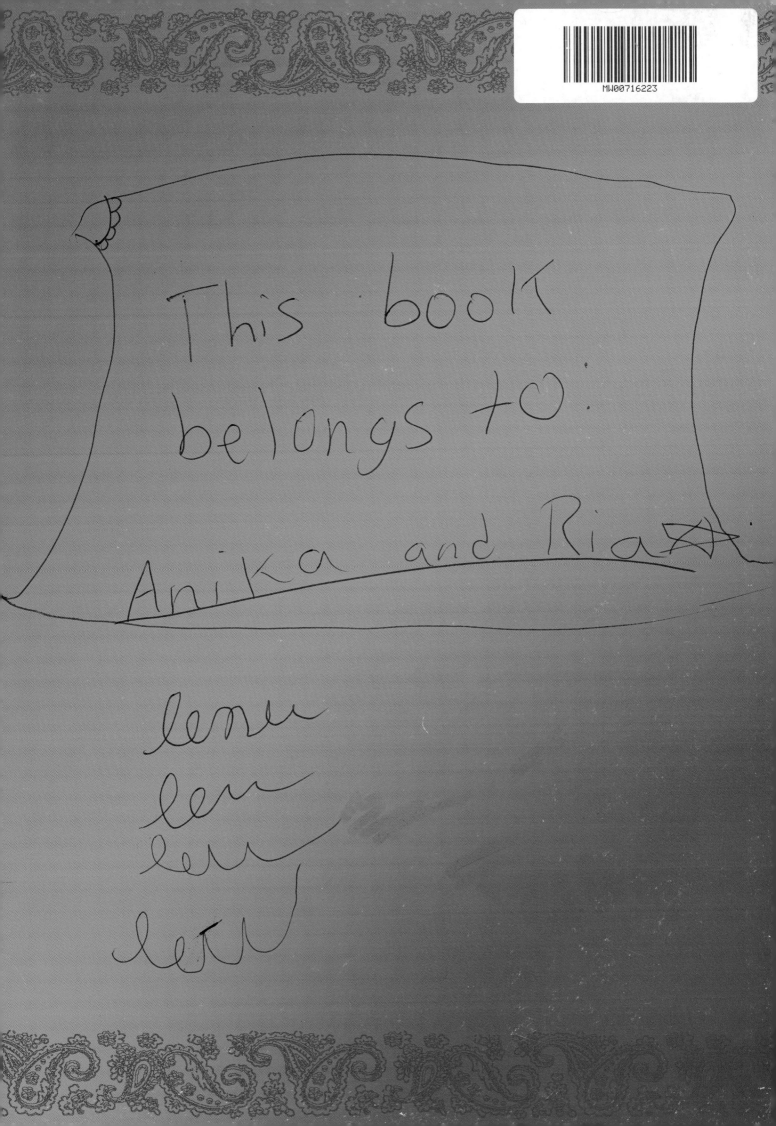

This book
belongs to:

Anika and Ria

India
My Land

STERLING

Sterling Publishers Private Limited
A-59, Okhla Indl. Area, Phase II, New Delhi 110020
Tel: (+91-11) 2638 6165; Fax: (+91-11) 2638 3788
E-mail: mail@sterlingpublishers.com
Website: www.sterlingpublishers.com

Printed at Sterling Publishers Pvt. Ltd., New Delhi

CONTENTS

Namaste!

In India, we believe that God resides in every being and so we bow down and join our hands in all humility and say *Namaste* or *Pranam* to greet each other. The action is not only a reverential gesture, it also signifies the unity of all souls.

THE NATIONAL FLAG

The national flag of India is a horizontal tricolour with deep saffron at the top, white in the middle and dark green at the bottom in equal proportions. The saffron stands for courage, sacrifice and the spirit of renunciation; the white, for purity and truth; the green, for faith and fertility. At the centre of the white band, there is a navy blue wheel with 24 spokes to indicate the *Dharma Chakra*, the Wheel of Law. The design of the national flag was adopted by India's Constituent Assembly on 22nd July, 1947.

THE NATIONAL ANTHEM

The Indian National anthem, composed originally in Bengali by Rabindranath Tagore, was adopted in its Hindi version by the Constituent Assembly as the National Anthem of India on 24th January 1950. The complete song consists of five stanzas. The lyrics were rendered into English by Tagore himself.

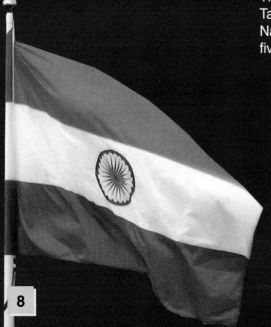

"Jana Gana Mana Adhinayaka Jaya Hae
Bharat Bhagya Vidhata
Punjab Sindh Gujarat Maratha
Dravida Utkala Banga
Vindhya Himachal Yamuna Ganga
Ucchala Jaladhi Taranga
Tava Shubha Name Jage
Tava Shubha Ashisha Mange
Gahe Tava Jaya Gatha
Jan Gan Mangaldayak Jaya He
Bharat Bhagya Vidhata
Jaya Hae! Jaya Hae! Jaya Hae!
Jaya, Jaya, Jaya, Jaya Hae!"

NATIONAL SYMBOLS OF INDIA

THE TIGER

The magnificent tiger is the national animal of India. The beautiful carnivore is a combination of grace, strength and power. In folklore and legends it is looked upon as the king of the jungle alternately ruthless and fierce or kind and just. These magnificent animals were indiscriminately hunted in the years preceding independence, drastically reducing their presence in the wild.

To check their dwindling population, which came down to just 1,827 in 1972, a massive conservation programme was initiated in April 1973, known as 'Project Tiger'. According to WWF, there are about 2,000 Royal Bengal tigers in the wild today, including 1,411 in India.

THE PEACOCK

The peacock is the national bird of India. A multihued shimmering blue with a fan-shaped crest of feathers, a white patch under the eye and a long, slender neck, it is the epitome of grace, pride and mysticism. It has a spectacular bronze-green train of around 200 elongated feathers, with each feather enhanced with an eye at its end. It is capable of extending its tail erect like a fan in ostentatious display to its mates.

The bird is mostly found in the dry semi-desert grasslands, scrub and deciduous forests and feeds on mainly seeds, but some also eat insects, fruits and reptiles.

THE LOTUS

The lotus is the national flower of India. It is an aquatic plant with wide floating leaves and bright aromatic flowers in white and pink which grow only in shallow waters.

According to Tantrism, the unfolding petals of the lotus signify the expansion of the soul. The flower symbolises purity, beauty, majesty, grace, fertility, wealth, richness, knowledge and serenity.

Dancing peacock

The Lotus

Bharatnatyam

The Bengal tiger

9

THE BANYAN TREE

Found in almost all the parts of India, the banyan tree is the national tree of India. It is an evergreen tree. Its branches spread out and send trunk-like roots to the ground in order to support itself.

Indians consider the Banyan tree as 'Kalpa Vriksha', the tree that fulfils wishes. The mighty banyan tree is considered immortal and has always been the focal point for the village communities in India.

- The official Sanskrit name for India is 'Bharat'.

- India used to be called Bharat even in the *Satya Yuga* (Golden Age).

- The name 'India' is derived from the River Indus, the valleys around which were the homes of the early settlers. The Aryan worshippers referred to the river Indus as the 'Sindhu'.

- The Persian invaders changed it to 'Hindi'. The name 'Hindustan' combines Sindhu and Hindu, and thus refers to 'the land of the Hindus'.

- Population of India: 1,166,079,217

- India has 28 states and 7 union territories.

States: Andhra Pradesh, Arunachal Pradesh, Assam, Bihar, Chhattisgarh, Goa, Gujarat, Haryana, Himachal Pradesh, Jammu and Kashmir, Jharkhand, Karnataka, Kerala, Madhya Pradesh, Maharashtra, Manipur, Meghalaya, Mizoram, Nagaland, Odisha, Punjab, Rajasthan, Sikkim, Tamil Nadu, Tripura, Uttaranchal, Uttar Pradesh, West Bengal

Union Territories: Andaman and Nicobar Islands, Chandigarh, Dadra and Nagar Haveli, Daman and Diu, Lakshadweep, Puducherry.

The banyan tree

THE MANGO

The mango is one of the most widely-cultivated fruits of the tropical world. This juicy, delicious fruit is a rich source of Vitamins A, C and D. In India, there are hundreds of varieties of mangoes in different sizes, shapes and colours.

The mango

10

THE NATIONAL EMBLEM

The national emblem of India is a replica of the Sarnath Lion Capital near Varanasi in Uttar Pradesh. The Lion Capital was erected in the 3rd Century BC by Emperor Ashoka to mark the spot where Lord Buddha first proclaimed his gospel.

It symbolises India's reaffirmation of its ancient commitment to world peace and goodwill. In the original, there are four lions standing back to back. The four lions (one hidden from view) rest on a circular abacus and symbolise power, courage and confidence. The abacus is girded by four smaller animals - guardians of the four directions: the lion of the north, the elephant of the east, the horse of the south, and the bull of the west. The abacus rests on a lotus in full bloom, exemplifying the fountainhead of life and creative inspiration. The motto 'Satyameva Jayate' inscribed below the emblem means 'truth alone triumphs'. Carved out of a single block of polished sandstone, the capital is crowned by the Dharma Chakra (the Wheel of Law).

Carved door with inlay work

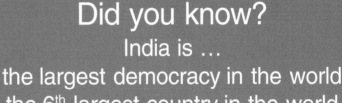

Did you know?
India is ...
the largest democracy in the world
the 6th largest country in the world
and one of the most ancient civilisations!

Indian elephant

11

Our Land

Elevation Extremes

Highest point: Mount Kanchenjunga (8,598 m)

Lowest point: Indian Ocean (0 m)

NSEW Extremes

North: Siachen Glacier in Jammu & Kashmir

South: Indira Point, the tip of Great Nicobar Island

East: Kibithu in Arunachal Pradesh

West: Ghuar Mota in Gujarat

Nagpur is practically at the geographical centre of India. In fact, the zero milestone of India is in this city!

The Baily Bridge is the highest bridge in the world, located in the Ladakh valley.

Drass in western Ladakh is the coldest place in India. It is also the second coldest place in the world.

India is such a vast country that the climate varies considerably – from tropical monsoon in south India to temperate in north India. While the heat is unbearable in the Thar Desert, the people of Ladakh and Kashmir shiver in the snowy cold.

The country sees four distinct seasons: winter from December to February, summer from March to May, the Southwest Monsoon from June to September and the post monsoon season, which is the Northeast monsoon in South India, in October and November.

There is heavy rainfall in the Northeastern region, the western slopes of the Western Ghats and parts of the Himalayas. Mawsynram in Meghalaya is the wettest place on Earth, with an annual rainfall of 11,872 mm. On the other hand, there is hardly any rainfall in Rajasthan, Kutch and Ladakh.

The Himalayas

The Himalayan range is considered as the world's highest mountain range (with its tallest peak Mt Everest), stretching from east to west, separating India from China and Nepal, and is often called 'the crown of India'. It is the source of the many rivers that drain the Northern plains that begin from its foothills.

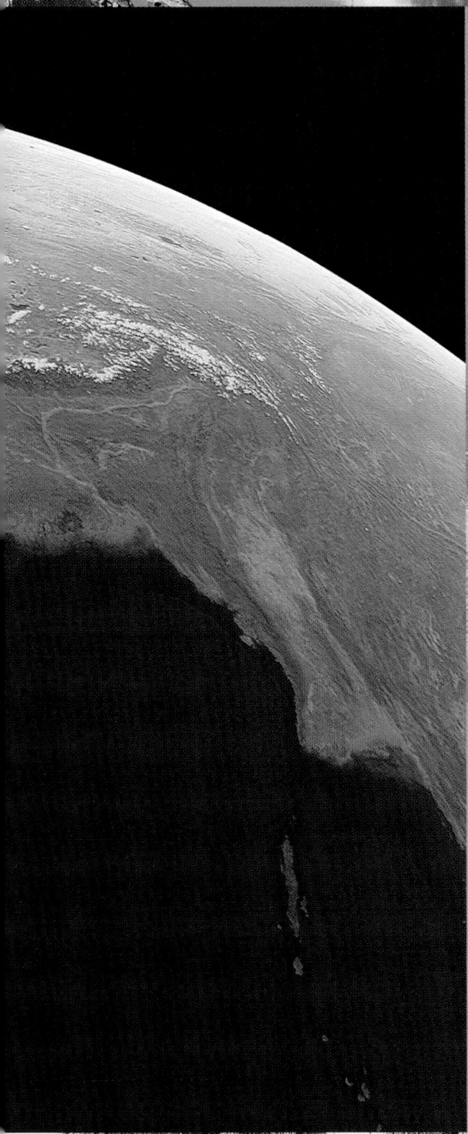

A Goa beach

The Northern plains are drained by a number of rivers making it a very fertile region. The rivers Ganga and Yamuna flow into the Bay of Bengal, and the river Indus into the Arabian Sea.

The Thar Desert, the seventh largest desert in the world, lies in Rajasthan. The Deccan Plateau spans most of central and south India. The Krishna, Godavari, Tungabhadra and Kaveri are the major rivers of the south.

The Ganga river

A boathouse in Kerala

Our People

Race/Ethnicity: Indo-Aryan 72%, Dravidian 25%, Mongoloid and other 3%

Population growth rate: 1.548%

Birth rate: 21.76 births/1,000 population

Infant mortality rate: 30.15 deaths/ 1,000 live births

Life expectancy: 69.89 years

Since time immemorial, India has been like a mother, treating all her children like one. It is a land, a nation where people of all religions, communities and cultures retain their individual identity and yet live together harmoniously. There are no restrictions on following one's heart when it comes to travelling through the country, or in choosing one's religious path or goal in life. People in this country cannot be classified into water tight compartments. It is this fluidity, this assimilation that is India.

Everyone who comes to this country becomes a part of it. India changes people, they say. If one were to talk about religious classification, there are many. Yet strong within them is the spirit of tolerance and respect for each other, which is the spirit of India.

Some who came or were brought to this country, never left. The people of Malana village of Kullu district in Himachal Pradesh are known for their Greek descent. They came with Alexander's army and remained here. Their features, language, religion and socio-economic structure resemble that of the ancient Greek civilisation. They manage their own judicial, social and religious lives and never vote, or marry outside their clan or take their matters to court.

Some residents of Goa who were Portuguese nationals before 1961, still retain that nationality and their votes for elections in Portugal are sent via mail.

Just as the people are varied, so are the attires typical to them. While women are traditionally known to wear sarees and *ghagra cholis*, men wear *dhotis* and *angavastra* or the latter day *dhoti kurta*. While young girls wear a long skirt and a blouse, teenaged girls couple the same with a *dupatta* draped around them and it is mainly the older women who wear sarees. The attractive and colourful attires worn by the people of the northeast are mainly hand-woven. In the northeastern states, the attire cannot be

generalised as easily as each tribe has a typical attire of its own. Women mostly wear a two-piece dress – one wrapped around like a long skirt and a shirt or top. The Bhutia women wear a *Honju* which is a loose, silken full sleeved blouse. The *Mekhala Chaddar* worn by Assamese women is a saree in two parts, usually woven in Muga and Pat Silk. The village women of Meghalaya wear the *Jyensyem*, two ankle-length pieces of cloth gathered at the shoulders and topped by a blouse.

The Sidis living in Gujarat, Karnataka, and Maharashtra, are descendants of Africans originally brought here through the heinous slave trade. Their presence in India can be traced to the early establishment of Muslim rule in the 13th-16th centuries. Today though their features differentiate them from others, they have become a part of the culture of where they live and converse in local languages.

However, as in all other countries economic disparities remain. The increasing gap between the two extremes is apparent even in their attire. While the cream vouches for brands like Armani, and Dolce Gabbana, the poor do not even have adequate clothes to wear. Still their zest for life and vibrant spirit is also a part of the spirit of India.

Our Cuisines

Indian cuisine is popular all over the world for its variety, mouth-watering tastes and aroma. Yet the country refuses to be defined and categorised, even in its cuisine. From the mouth-watering *Goshtaba* of Kashmir to the spicy *sambhar-dosa* of Kerala, the wholesome *Daalbhaati churma* of Rajasthan to the *dimsums* and *thukpas* of Meghalaya, the cuisine is as varied as the country's people.

Every cuisine is born from the innovative use of ingredients available locally. In the olden times, it was also affected by the particular tastes of the king or the royal family, the prevalent religion, the army of invaders and the numerous settlers from foreign countries.

The Hindu and the Muslim traditions have influenced Indian cooking. Over time, their indigenous styles blended seamlessly to form a new cuisine. By the influence of Muslims, northern India saw the birth of Mughlai cuisine. The Portuguese had their influence on the cuisine in Goa.

Some of the more famous cuisines are the Mughlai, Chettinad, Hyderabadi and Punjabi styles of cooking. Spices are an essential element of Indian cuisine, though the combination of spices used are typical to each region. Different kinds of oil, butter and clarified butter (*ghee*) are the medium of cooking. While rice is the staple food in south and northeast India, the rest of the country consumes plain breads like *rotis, paranthas*, *kulchas*, and deep fried ones like *puris* and *bhatooras*.

Sweets are usually milk based. While sweets such as g*ulab jamun*, *laddoo* and *jalebi* are ubiquitous, many others like *rasbhari*, *peda*, *burfi*, *malpua* and *rasgulla* are local favourites.

The rich sauces, butter-based curries, and ginger-flavoured roast meats of northern India make it very popular worldwide. *Kababs, kormas, naans* and *tandoori* chicken are typical of the style.

The *samosa* is a very popular snack filled with boiled, mashed potato. Popular snacks, side-dishes and drinks include *pakoda, bhujiya, chaat, kachori, imarti,* several types of pickles, *murabba, sharbat, aam panna* and *aam papad.*

Samosas

South Indian cuisine is best known for the *dosa, idli* and *vada, sambar, rasam,* and *aviyal.* Coconut oil is the main medium of cooking and tamarind, coconut and curry leaves are liberally used.

Hyderabadi cuisine, largely influenced by the rich food of the Nizams, is another charming facet of South Indian cuisine.

Chettinad cuisine is hot and pungent with fresh ground spices, and topped with a boiled egg.

Udupi cuisine is strictly vegetarian. The *masala dosa* had its origin in Udupi.

Thali meal

Traditional cuisines of Odisha, Bengal and Assam are delicately spiced. Mustard oil is the preferred medium of cooking. Fish and rice are the staple food of the region.

East Indian cuisine is famous for its desserts, especially sweets such as *rasgulla, chumchum, sandesh, chhena poda, chhena gaja, chhena jalebi* and *kheer.*

Gujarati cuisine is primarily vegetarian with a distinctive combination of sweet, salty, and spicy flavours at the same time.

Jalebis

Maharashtrian cuisine depends more on rice, coconut, and fish. Goan cuisine is mainly delicious seafood and rice with generous use of coconut milk, and kokum is another distinct feature.

Popular sweets are known as *mithai,* such as *gulab jamun, jalebi, peda, petha, rewadi, gajak, singori, kulfi, falooda, ras malai, gulkand,* and several varieties of *laddu, barfi* and *halwa.*

Chicken curry

17

Indian sweets

Our Religions

Many religions have been founded in India: Hinduism, Sikhism, Buddhism and Jainism. The Muslims, Parsees, Jews and the Tibetans in exile were welcomed with open arms because of the ancient Hindu belief that the whole world is one family. All these religions peacefully coexist in India. No religious thought was ever trampled upon in this country.

Aum is the most sacred word in the Hindu scriptures. The *Mandukya Upanishad* is entirely devoted to explaining it. The three phonemes, *a*, *u* and *m*, are seen as symbolising the three *Vedas* or the Hindu Trinity.

Sadhus

In any *yajna* or ceremony, or before embarking on any new project, the elephant god Ganesha is to be prayed to first, as he is the remover of all obstacles. The principal scriptures dedicated to Ganesha are the *Ganesha Purana*, the *Mudgala Purana*, and the *Ganapati Atharvashirsa*.

Buddhism was founded by Gautama Buddha in the sixth century BC. He delivered his first sermon in the Deer park in Sarnath. He prescribed the Path of Eightfold Virtue: Right views, Right speech, Right action, Right living, Right effort, Right resolve, Right recollection and Right meditation. The Sarnath pillar, the frescoes in the Ajanta Caves and the *Dharma Chakra* of Emperor Ashoka are famous instances of Buddhist art and architecture. *Mahayana*, *Hinayana* and *Vajrayana* are the three sects of Buddhism.

Jainism was founded by Lord Mahavira in the seventh century BC. Mahavira preached self control, non-violence, simple life, detachment, non-possession and pluralism with diverse thinking, known as *Anekantavada*. The Jains are divided into two main sects, *Swetambaras* and *Digambaras*.

Sikhism was founded in the fifteenth century by Guru Nanak Dev in Punjab. He regarded ritual, idolatory, caste, genocide and the

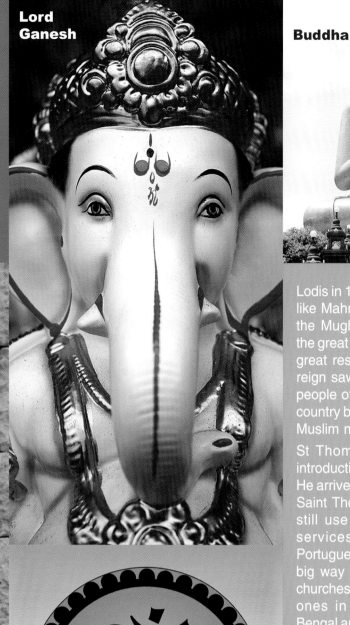

Lord Ganesh

Buddha

Lodis in 1526. Unlike other invaders like Mahmud of Ghazni and Ghori, the Mughals came to stay. Akbar, the great Mughal emperor accorded great respect to Hinduism and his reign saw an easy commingling of people of both religions. Today our country boasts of the world's largest Muslim minority population.

St Thomas is credited with the introduction of Christianity in India. He arrived in Malabar in 52 AD. The Saint Thomas Christians in Kerala still use the Syriac language in services. The French and the Portuguese spread Christianity in a big way in India. The Portuguese churches in Old Goa and the French ones in Pondicherry and West Bengal are remnants of those times.

In a series of migrations from the seventh century onwards, the Parsees arrived in India. They are followers of Zarathustra and their earliest written scripture is the *Zend Avesta*.

The Constitution of India declares the nation to be a secular republic.

Aum – religious symbol

destruction of religious monuments as against the beliefs of both Hinduism an Islam. By the time that he left for his heavenly abode, the new religion had already taken root. He was followed by ten successive Gurus, the last Guru being the Guru Granth Sahib. Sikhism is the fifth-largest organised religion in the world.

Islam arrived in India with the Mughal invasion and defeat of the

Muslims at prayer

19

The **Jama Masjid** of Delhi, is the biggest mosque in India. It was begun by Shah Jahan in 1650 and completed six years later and cost about a million rupees. The courtyard of the mosque can hold up to twenty-five thousand worshippers.

The **Church of Bom Jesus** 'Good' or 'Infant Jesus' is well known originally for the tomb of St Francis Xavier. This church is one of the richest churches in Goa and is carpeted with marble flooring and inlaid with precious stones.

The world-renowned **Khajuraho Temples** are in Madhya Pradesh. The walls of the shrines are covered with exquisite sculptures depicting the tales and characters in the various *Puranas*.

The **Badrinath** temple, dedicated to god Vishnu, is situated at the confluence of the Alaknanda and the Rishi Ganga. An ancient pilgrimage centre, it has attracted pilgrims for centuries both for its religious value and its natural grandeur.

Church of Bom Jesus in Goa

The **Great Stupa** at Sanchi was originally commissioned by the emperor Ashoka the Great in the third century BC. Its nucleus was a simple hemispherical brick structure built over the relics of the Buddha. It was crowned by the *chatra*, a parasol-like structure symbolising high rank, which was intended to honour and shelter the relics.

Haridwar is known as the gate of the abode of Shiva to the plains. The evening aarti at Har Ki Paori when Ganga Mata is worshipped is mesmerising.

Sanchi Stupa

Kapaleeshwara Temple

Evening aarti, Haridwar

20

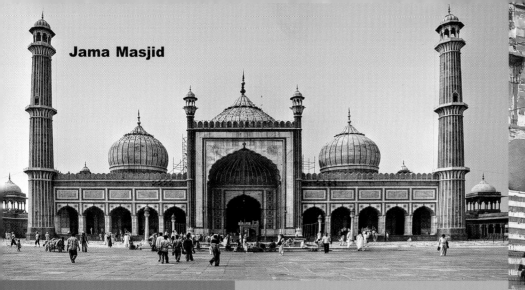

Jama Masjid

Lotus Temple

Varanasi is a holy city on the banks of the Ganga. It is said that those who are cremated here attain *moksha* or liberation.

The **Lotus Temple** is the last of the seven major Baha'i temples built around the world. The Baha'I faith believes in the oneness of all religions and mankind. The architect chose the lotus as a symbol common to Hinduism, Buddhism, Jainism and Islam.

Varanasi

Golden Temple

The **Golden Temple** or Harmandir Sahib, in Amritsar, is the most sacred shrine of the Sikhs and is over 200 years old.

The **Birla Mandir** is dedicated to Vishnu and his consort Lakshmi. Located in Delhi, it is the first of the temples built across the country by the industrial family of the Birlas. Built in 1938, it was inaugurated by Mahatma Gandhi on the express condition that people of all castes and especially untouchables would be allowed in. The condition is followed to this day.

The **Hanuman Temple** in Madhya Pradesh,was built by the then Orchha ruler, Raja Sujan Singh. The monarchs of Orchha were great devotees of Lord Rama and built monuments in memory of almost all the important characters in the epic Ramayana.

Our Festivals

Festivals are a time to get together, to share, to relive happy times, and rejuvenate oneself. They are celebrations, reminders of the triumph of truth, integrity and valour, the vindication of the words of prophets and seers, the proof of man's gratitude and hope in the face of a cruel, despondent world. They are signs of man's belief in God and his minions. Indians celebrate all festivals with great verve. With a pantheon of 33 million Hindu gods and goddesses, and the holy days of all the other religions that coexist in this country, it is hardly a wonder that each day is a festival! A number of these festivals revolve around Lord Rama.

The main festival season for the Hindus begins with the Navratri, concluding with **Dussehra**. The battle between Rama and Ravana lasted ten days and ended on the tenth day with the vanquishing of Ravana, and thus the other name *Vijayadashami*, for the festival. Most Hindus fast on these nine days and *Ramalila* is enacted through out the country. Lord Rama also invoked the martial Goddess Durga to triumph over the arch demon and thus **Durga Puja** is also celebrated at this time. She is also said to come home for a visit at this time and also to annihilate the demon Mahishasura. She returns home on the tenth day, Dussehra.

After Lord Ram's triumph over Ravana, his return to Ayodhya after 14 years is celebrated on **Diwali**. On Diwali, all houses are decorated with flowers and are brightly lit to welcome the goddess Lakshmi, and the elephant god Ganesh, signifying the prosperity and well-being that Lord Rama brings with him. Only in West Bengal is the goddess Kali worshipped along with goddess Lakshmi on this day.

Pongal is a harvest festival celebrated in Tamil Nadu, Andhra Pradesh and Karnataka.

Onam is the harvest festival celebrated in Kerala. The snake boat race held in the pristine lagoons is a breathtaking sight.

Baisakhi is celebrated with great zest in Punjab.

The Parsis celebrate their new year **Jamshed Navroz** according to the Fasli calendar.

Holi is the festival of rioutous colours and revelry. The cheerful bonfires remind onlookers of the way Prahlad's devotion saved him from the jaws of death.

Vasanta Panchami is celebrated in Haryana and Punjab as the end of winter. In West Bengal and Odisha this festival is a celebration of the goddess of learning Saraswati.

The marriage and the unity of Shiva and Parvati is a theme of many festivals. **Gangaur** is celebrated in Rajasthan to invoke the blessings of Goddess Parvati, on young maidens so that they too may find a husband like Lord Shiva.

In Madurai, **Meenakshi Kalyanam** is celebrated each year to celebrate the marriage of Meenakshi with Lord Shiva.

Teej is celebrated with great gusto by women in Rajasthan. The birth anniversary of Lord Krishna, is celebrated as **Janmashtami**.

Christmas celebrated on December 25, commemorates the birth of Jesus Christ. Santa Claus is a popular mythological figure, associated with bringing gifts for children.

The birthday of Guru Nanak is celebrated as **Guru Purab**.

The birth of Mahavira, the last Tirthankara is celebrated as **Mahavir Jayanti**.

The birth anniversary of the Lord Buddha is celebrated as **Buddha Purnima** or **Buddha Jayanti**. He not only attained enlightenment on this day, he also attained 'Nirvana' or left the mortal world.

The birth anniversary of Prophet Zarathushtra is celebrated as **Khordad Sal**.

The Muslim festival **Id-ul-Fitr** marks the end of the month of Ramzan. It is an occasion for feasting and rejoicing and offering prayers. The occasion of **Muharram** commemorates the martyrdom of Imam Hussain.

Our Monuments

Taj Mahal

Monuments inscribed on the UNESCO World Heritage List

Taj Mahal (1983), Agra Fort (1983), Ajanta Caves (1983), Ellora Caves (1983), Sun Temple, Konarak (1984), Group of Monuments at Mahabalipuram (1984), Churches and Convents of Goa (1986), Fatehpur Sikri (1986), Group of Monuments at Hampi (1986), Khajuraho Group of Monuments (1986), Elephanta Caves (1987), Group of Monuments at Pattadakal (1987), Great Living Chola Temples (1987), Buddhist Monuments at Sanchi (1989), Humayun's Tomb, Delhi (1993), Qutub Minar and its monuments, Delhi (1993), Mountain Railways of India (1999), Mahabodhi Temple Complex at Bodh Gaya (2002), Rock Shelters of Bhimbetka (2003), Champaner-Pavagadh Archaeological Park (2004), Chhatrapati Shivaji Terminus (2004), Red Fort Complex (2007)

Monuments, ruins in stone that kings left for posterity. Some like the Taj Mahal have remained unscathed for centuries, others were ravaged by invaders, wars and the endless tides of time. The Indus Valley Civilisation was known as the 'cradle of the world' and its ruins and monuments are still standing. India has a stupendous array of ancient monuments, influenced by many religions and cultures; from the ancient temples of Chamba, the Ajanta, Ellora and Elephanta caves, the Shore temple of Mahabalipuram, the Charminar in Hyderabad and the churches of Old Goa.

The **Taj Mahal** is a mausoleum located in Agra, India that evokes the love of Emperor Shah Jahan for his wife Mumtaz Mahal. The Mughal architecture exemplified in this structure is a combination of Persian, Indian and Islamic styles. The building began around 1632 and was completed around 1653. In 1983, the Taj Mahal was designated a UNESCO World Heritage Site and was cited as 'the jewel of Muslim art in India and one of the universally admired masterpieces of the world's heritage'.

Jantar Mantar

Qutub Minar

The **Jantar Mantar** was built in 1710 by Raja Jai Singh II of Jaipur in Delhi. It is an observatory consisting of mason-built astronomical instruments to chart the course of the heavens. The *yantras* (instruments, which locals distorted to Jantar) are built of brick rubble and plastered with lime. It can tell the time to the accuracy of 2 seconds!

The **Qutub Minar** was built by Qutub-ud-din Aibak. It stands next to the Quwwat-ul-Islam mosque and was probably built for the priest to climb up to call the faithful for prayer. It could also have been built as a tower of victory.

India Gate

India Gate, the All India War Memorial, was built in the memory of the 90,00 soldiers who laid down their lives during World War I. Located at Rajpath, New Delhi, it was designed and constructed by Lutyens. It is 42 m high and stands tall above Amar Jawan Jyoti (the flame of the immortal warrior) which is always burning to remind the nation of soldiers who perished in the Indo-Pakistan War of 1971.

Red Fort (Delhi)

Victorial Memorial

The **Victoria Memorial** in Kolkata is a memorial of Queen Victoria opened by the Prince of Wales in 1921. It houses some of the memorabilia of the British Raj and personal effects of Queen Victoria.

Jaisalmer Fort in Rajasthan is one of the largest forts in the world. Its massive yellow sandstone walls are a golden colour during the day and gain an alluring honey-gold as the sun sets, thus the name Golden Fort. About a quarter of the city's population live in it.

Rashtrapati Bhawan

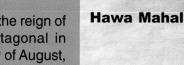

Hawa Mahal

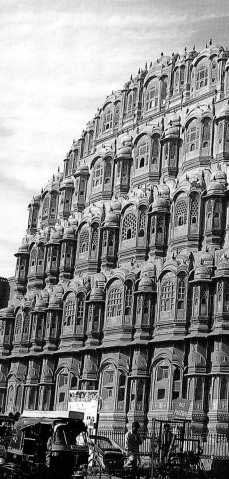

The **Lal Qila** was built during the reign of Shah Jahan. The fort is octagonal in shape. Every year, on the 15th of August, as the nation celebrates its independence, the National Flag of India is hoisted here by the Prime Minister.

The **Rashtrapati Bhawan** is often looked upon as one of the most significant creations of Lutyens. At that time it cost a whopping £12, 53, 000 and now is the official residence of the President of India. The sprawling monument gracefully adorns the crown of Raisina Hill and is the focal point of New Delhi.

Shore Temple

The **Shore Temple** in Mahabalipuram is a UNESCO World Heritage Site. Built by Narasimhavarman II, it is a five-storeyed structural temple, built with blocks of granite, dating from the 8th century AD. The temple has two shrines placed one behind the other, one facing east and the other west with a rectangular shrine sandwiched in between. The two shrines are dedicated to Shiva, while the one in between is dedicated to Vishnu.

Inspired by Persian architecture, **Humayun's Tomb** was the first garden tomb in the Indian subcontinent. It was the first to use the unique combination of red sandstone and white marble. It was built by the orders of Hamida Banu Begum, his widow, nine years after his death.

Purana Qila

Charminar

Humayun's Tomb

The **Purana Qila** was the inner citadel of the city of Dina-panah, founded by the second Mughal Emperor, Humayun. The fort has three massive arched gateways. Only a few of the interior structures have survived except the Qila-i Kuhna Mosque and the Shermandal, both credited to Sher Shah Suri.

The **Charminar** in Hyderabad, so called because of its four minarets, was built by Sultan Muhammad Quli Qutub Shah to commemorate the elimination of a plague epidemic from this city.

Parliament House

Situated to the northwest of Vijay Chowk, the **Parliament House** is a huge, circular, colonnaded building comprising three semicircular chambers for the Legislatures and a Central Library crowned by a 27.4m high dome. Earlier it was called the Circular House.

The **Hawa Mahal**, or the Palace of Winds, is arguably Jaipur's best-known monument. Made of red sandstone, it gives the city its name of Pink City. It was built for the ladies of the court to observe everyday life on the streets, without being seen themselves. Executed with intricate detail, with spacious jharokhas and natural cooling, it is an enigma in the midst of a bustling city.

Our Dances

India boasts of a wide range of dance forms from the ancient classical dance forms, to folk dances and the more modern Bollywood style influenced by Latino and Salsa. India has eight classical dance forms: Bharatnatyam, Kathak, Odissi, Kuchupudi, Mohiniattam, Kathakali, Sattriya and Manipuri.

Kathak originated in northern India. Traditionally, wandering storytellers who would act and sing to entertain people were called Kathaks. This crude form received Central Asian influence in the Mughal court and acquired a distinct form. The most important exponent of this style today is Birju Maharaj of the Maharaj family of dancers.

Odissi originated in the coastal state, Odisha. This dance form distinguishes itself from the others in the independent movement of head, chest and pelvis. Kelucharan Mahapatra revived this dance form in the 20th century and was the best known exponent of the dance form. The renowned dancers Sanjukta Panigrahi and Sonal Mansingh, were both his disciples.

Sattriya originated in the northeastern state, Assam and has had a continuous tradition since its inception in the fifteenth century. It was meant to accompany one act plays enacted in the monasteries (*Sattras*) in the region, hence the name.

In the present day, it is performed as an independent dance form. Menaka and Indira PP Bora are famous exponents of this form.

Bharatnatyam originated in Tamil Nadu. Traditionally it was a solo dance, performed by *devadasis* in temples as a way of greeting and reverence to the deities. Rukmini Devi Arundale was instrumental in bringing it to the attention of the West.

Manipuri originated in Manipur. The unique feature of the dance form is the use of cymbals by female dancers and of a double-headed drum by the male dancers.

Mudra

Bharatnatyam

Mohiniattam originated in Kerala as a graceful dance performed as a solo recital by women. Unlike Bharatnatyam, where the arch deity is Shiva, in this form the deity is Vishnu when he takes the form an alluring woman Mohini to save the gods from wily demons. The main theme of the dance is love and devotion to God, with usually Vishnu or Krishna being the hero.

Kathakali is an ancient form of dance-drama that originated in Kerala. It is unique in its intricate make-up for different characters and its elaborate costumes and head gears. Renowned Kathakali exponents today include Kalamandalam Ramankutty Nair and Madavoor Vasudevan Nair.

Mudras are gestures that were part of the ancient yogic practices and each basic *mudra* has a meaning attached to it. The gestures made with one hand are called *Asamyukta Hastah*. Gestures formed by uniting both hands are called *Samyukta Hastah*.

Nataraja

Nataraja, or the Lord of Dance, is an ancient depiction of Lord Shiva dancing in the midst of flames, standing on the demon Apasmara who symbolizes ignorance and evil.

There are numerous folk dances in India, each typical to a region, community or tribe like the Bhangra of Punjab, the Garba and Dandiya of Gujarat, the Bihu of Assam, the Hikal of Himachal Pradesh, Chhau of Bihar and the Hajgiri of Tripura.

Kathakali

29

Our Music

Indian classical music harks back to a hoary past where the *Sama Veda*, the second of the four *Vedas* was sung and not recited. *Sama Veda* enumerates seven notes. The scale of the seven notes given in the *Sama Veda* is known as a *Saptak*. There are six *ragas* and thirty-six *raginis*. The *ragas* can be used according to season or the time of day. For example, *Raga Hori-kafee* depicts the splash of colours in nature after severe winters, *Raga Basant*, the full bloom of spring and *Raga Malhar* the monsoon clouds and rains.

There are two main streams of music in India: the Hindustani classical and Carnatic. While Carnatic music is completely based on the traditions of the *Vedas*, Hindustani classical music was influenced by Central Asian styles and has the lighthearted *thumri* and *tappa*.

Harmonium

Bhakti music among the Hindus and Qawwali among the Sufis are two forms of folk music prevalent in India. While the Bhakti singers use the *ektara* or *dotara*, the *qawwals* use the harmonium, *tabla* and *dholak*. The Bauls of Bengal are known as wanderers in search of truth and mostly seen with the *ektara*.

Pandit Bhimsen Joshi is a legendary practitioner of Hindustani Classical music. He is a world renowned vocalist and known throughout the world as a stalwart in his field. M S Subbulakshmi, was a spellbinding exponent of the Carnatic style and was known as the nightingale of India.

Sitar

Tabla

India has a whole horde of plucked stringed instruments from the mighty seven-stringed *Rudra veena* to the humble single stringed *Ektara*. The *Rudra veena* and *Vichitra veena* are mostly used with Carnatic Music. The sitar is mostly used with Hindustani Classical Music. Pandit Ravi Shankar is the most exemplary performer on this instrument.

The *tabla* is one of the most popular percussion instruments used in Hindustani classical music.

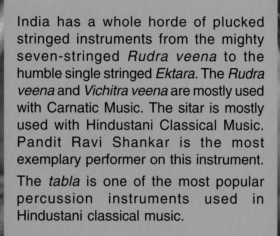

Ustad Alla Rakha and his son Zakir Hussain Qureishi are the classical tabla virtuosos of the country.

The *dholak* is a double-headed hand-drum. It is either played on the player's lap or, while standing, slung from the shoulder or waist. The shell is usually made by hollowing out *shisham* wood and used in everyday functions.

Dholak

The *bansuri*, or flute, occupies pride of place in Indian music as it is the favourite of Lord Krishna. Pandit Hariprasad Chaurasia is a famous flautist of the country.

The harmonium though not indigenous to India, has become ubiquitous here. It is used in the devotional singing of prayers, be it *bhajan*, *kirtan* or *qawwali*.

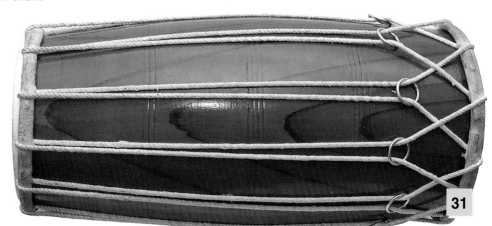

Art and Cinema

Much has been said about art being the product of the leisure of a developed civilisation, but the earliest extant cave paintings defy such theories. The earliest cave paintings in Bhimbetka, Madhya Pradesh take us back to prehistoric times. The spellbinding frescoes and murals of Ajanta and Ellora were painted in the 7th century and continue to attract tourists by the hordes. Changing tastes of the rulers, new religions and foreign influences ensured a healthy growth and amalgamation of styles.

Miniature painting emerged in India in the 11th-12th centuries. These were etched on palm leaf manuscripts and depicted Buddhist and Jaina sories.

Folk art

While the trend of such paintings continued, the Mughal era (16th-19th centuries) saw a unique blend of Indian, Persian and Islamic styles, later described as the Mughal School of Miniature Paintings.

In the 18th century, the proud Rajputs evolved their own style of miniature paintings. But more famous today are the paintings and frescoes that adorn the walls of their ancient *havelis*. The Shekhawati region, especially district Jhunjhunu is known for many such paintings on display.

While the northern regions were thus influenced, the southern parts of the country were left relatively untouched and the two main styles of painting from those regions are the Mysore and the Tanjore schools of painting. Both styles largely depict Hindu Gods and Goddesses.

Post Independence, Western influences made an impact on Indian painting. Some of the more famous painters today are M F Hussain, Tyeb Mehta, Akbar Padamsee, Jamini Roy and Jatin Das.

Puppetry is a traditional form of entertainment. Kerala has two forms: the *Tolpavakuthu* or shadow puppets and the *Pavakathakali* or glove-puppets. The rest of the country has string puppets, like the *Kathputli* of Rajasthan, the *Gombeatta* of Karnataka, the *Gopalila Kundhei* of Odisha and the *Kalasutri* Bahuliya of Maharashtra.

Katputhli

According to the Guiness Book of World Records the largest film studio complex in the world is the Ramoji Film City in Hyderabad! The famous Madame Tussauds wax museum houses wax figures of Bollywood greats Amitabh Bachchan, Shah Rukh Khan, Salman Khan and Aishwarya Rai Bachchan.

While most of the audience is attracted to commercial cinema with melodrama, song and dance sequences and action scenes, the 'Parallel Cinema' movement, has also been very strong in India. Directors like Satyajit Ray, Ritwik Ghatak and Shyam Benegal are exemplars of this form.

In the 21st century, Indian cinema went global. Enhanced technology paved the way for upgradation from established cinematic norms. Indian cinema found markets in over 90 countries and there was participation in international film festivals. Indian filmmakers such as Shekhar Kapur, Mira Nair, Deepa Mehta, etc. found success overseas.

India took its first step in cinema with the first short film *The Flower of Persia* in 1898. The renowned scholar Dadasaheb Phalke produced *Raja Harishchandra*, the first full-length motion picture in India in 1913. *Alam Ara*, the first Indian talking film, was released on 14 March 1931.

Today the Indian cinema industry is the world's largest producer of films, producing almost over a thousand films each year. Along with Bollywood films, Telugu films account for about 600 films a year, while the rest of the regional languages notch up the rest.

Khajuraho Temple art

Architecture and sculpture also flourished in the country. Some of the many famous examples of religious architecture are the Tabo Monastery in Spiti Valley, the Shore Temple in Mahabalipuram, and the Khajuraho group of temples in Madhya Pradesh. The Khajuraho group of temples were built over a span of 200 years and are world renowned for the religious and secular sculptures on the walls of the temples.

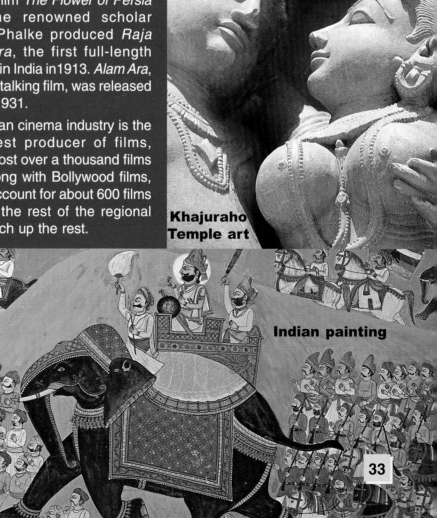

Indian painting

Our Literature

Indian mythology abounds with tales of *devas* (demigods) and *asuras* (demons) and the continuing struggle between them. They are mostly symbolic of the ongoing struggle between good and evil inside every human being. However, Hindus only have two famous epics, the *Ramayana* and the *Mahabharata*.

The creation of the *Mahabharata* is attributed to sage Ved Vyasa. It is an epic tale narrating the conflict between the Pandavas and the Kauravas. The *Ramayana* is a Sanskrit epic by Maharshi Valmiki, depicting the life and times of Lord Rama, son of King Dasharatha of Ayodhya.

Even though the two epics centre round different themes, they are essentially ways of communicating the ideals of righteous conduct (*Dharma*).

These epics are an intrinsic part of Hindu philosophy and everyday life and many children are still named after the heroes and heroines of these epics.

Kalidasa penned two epics, *Raghuvamsha*, *Kumarasambhava*, and the lyrical poem, *Meghaduta*. *Raghuvamsha* tells the story of the family of Dileepa and his descendants, including that of the brave conqueror Raghu. *Kumarasambhava* is an epic of penance and love. The name literally means 'Birth of Kumara', i.e. Kartikeya, the valiant son of Shiva and Parvati. This epic describes how Parvati first undergoes penance to win Shiva's love and the love between them that gives birth to Kartikeya who alone can kill the demon Tarakasur. *Meghaduta*, another short lyrical poem by the poet is one of his most famous works. It describes how an exiled yaksa convinces a passing cloud to carry his message to his wife. The language used in all three was classical Sanskrit as it was the language used by the royal family at that time.

Cilappatikaram is one of the most important Tamil epics. It depicts the power of the chaste woman Kannagi, who by virtue of being a loyal and chaste wife true to her *Dharma*, has the power to invoke the wrath of the gods and punish the evil forces, however powerful.

Written by Tulsidas, *Ramacharita-manasa*, based on the life and deeds of Prince Rama was the first epic to appear in Hindi. He gave a human character to Rama, portraying him as an ideal son, husband, brother and king.

Mirza Ghalib is regarded as one of the greatest Urdu Poets. Ghalib's poetry is distinguished by its intense feelings, wistfulness and a strong romantic mood which produce a charming effect on readers.

'Diwan-i-Ghalibin', a collection of his poetic works, has been translated into several Indian and foreign languages. As a writer and poet, Ghalib believed in using simple words. He laid the foundation of Urdu prose and that is why he is called the father of modern Urdu prose.

Rabindranath Tagore was a writer and painter of great note. In 1901, he founded the Vishwa-Bharati University in West Bengal with the aim of evolving a world culture, a synthesis of eastern and western values. Our National Anthem 'Jana Gana Mana' was written by him.

He won the Nobel Prize for literature in 1913 for his collection of poems 'Gitanjali'.

Munshi Premchand was the most famous Hindi novelist. Renowned poets include Ramdhari Singh 'Dinkar', Maithili Sharan Gupt, Agyeya and Harivansh Rai Bachchan.

A new breed of writers began the trend of Indians writing in English. Writers include: R. K. Narayan, Vikram Seth, Arundhati Roy, Amitav Ghosh, Rohinton Mistry, Khushwant Singh, Shashi Tharoor, Nayantara Sehgal, Anita Desai, Kiran Desai, Kamala Das, Ashok Banker and many others.

Kannada epic poetry mainly consists of Jain religious literature. Asaga wrote *Vardhaman Charitra (Life of Vardhaman Mahavir)*, the first biography of the 24th and last Tirthankara of Jainism.

Adikavi Pampa wrote *Vikramarjuna Vijaya*, also called *Pampa Bharata*, an adaptation of the *Mahabharata*, the first such adaptation in Kannada.

Lord Rama, Sita and Laxmana

Yoga and Martial Arts

Kalaripayattu

The world has drawn sustenance from India in myriad ways including Yoga, the science of attuning the mind and body with the Creator, and martial art forms, the invention of a proud people in the face of war.

Yoga is an amalgamation of ancient Indian philosophy aimed at uniting the mind and body to attain oneness with the absolute. It brings together traditional physical and mental disciplines. Of the many textual sources for the same are the middle *Upanishads*, the *Mahabharata*, especially the *Bhagavad Gita* and the *Yoga Sutras* of Patanjali.

Through the ages, the physical practice of *asanas* and *pranayama* have been largely advocated in Indian households. In recent years, Baba Ramdev has shot to fame because of the way in which he has popularised and advocated *pranayama* and *yogasanas*.

Other ways of encouraging physical fitness was to do it with the practice of various martial art forms. In Sanskrit, one finds terms for archery and the use of other weapons. While various parts of southern India saw the rise of *Kalaripayattu* as a martial art form, northern India witnessed *Mallayuddha* or wrestling, and regional forms like *Gatka* in Punjab and *Thang-Ta* in Manipur.

A number of inputs like the location of the 107 vital points of the human body were taken from the 4th century *Sushruta Samhita* that formed the basis for Ayurveda, the Indian system of medicine. Of the 107, 64 were classified as being lethal if properly struck with a fist or stick, and are still in use in martial art forms the world over. The *Agni Purana* enumerates 9 basic *asanas* or positions of standing in a fight.

Kalaripayattu is still practiced in Kerala and contiguous regions. As in any other form of martial arts, this form includes grappling, kicks, strikes and healing methods. While it can be traced back to the second or even third century BC, it was banned by the British in 1804 and saw revival only in the 1920s. The practice of this form transcended gender, caste and communal lines. Three main schools of practice can be distinguished in this martial art form. The northern style places more emphasis on weapons than on empty hands. The central style has its own distinct moves performed within floor drawings. The southern style emphasises the uses of empty hands rather than weapons.

The Sikhs are known to be a martial race and *gatka* is a martial art form practiced by them. Though the curved and straight swords are the main weapons used in this martial art form, the other weapons used are: Kirpan, Lathi, whips, chains, knife, bow and arrow, spear, and *chakram*.

Thang-Ta or huyen lallong is a weapon-based martial art that originated in Manipur. The sword and the spear are the primary weapons used in this style.

Sarit Sarak, also developed in Manipur, is the art of fighting empty-handed against armed or unarmed opponents. Being designed more for self defence than for attack it emphasises on evasive tactics.

Martial arts were banned during the British occupation of the region, but the 1950s saw a resurgence of the traditional fighting forms.

In 2009, Gurumayum Gourakishor Sharma, a leading exponent and teacher of Thang-Ta, received the Padma Shri honour for his contributions to the advancement of Thang-Ta.

Famous Indians

Forerunners

Rabindranath Tagore was the first Indian to win the Nobel Prize. He received the Nobel Prize for Literature in 1913, for his collection of poems, *Gitanjali*.

Ajeet Bajaj is the first Indian to go to both North and South Poles. He performed this feat in 2007.

Sarojini Naidu became the first Indian woman to be made the Governor of a state in 1947.

Vijay Lakshmi Pandit was not only the first Indian, but also the first woman president of the United Nations General Assembly in 1953.

Laxmi Narayan Mitttal is the richest Indian and 4th in the Forbes Top 100 Billionaires of the World list.

Mahatma Gandhi

Manmohan Singh, best known as 'father of liberalisation' is the Prime Minister of India. He is the first Prime Minister since Jawaharlal Nehru to return to power after completing a full five-year term. He is hailed as the cleanest man in Indian politics.

Manmohan Singh held several positions throughout the 1980s and early 1990s. An academician, he was discovered by former Prime Minister Shri P V Narasimha Rao, who offered him the Finance Ministry in 1991 under the Congress Government. During his stint as the Finance Minister (1991-1996), the suave, soft-spoken Sikh guided India out of financial trouble and put the country on course to becoming an economic power by opening up the economy to foreign investment.

Mother Teresa was an Albanian Catholic nun who came to India and founded the Missionaries of Charity in Kolkata. She dedicated herself to the service of mankind and served God amongst the poorest of the poor, the sick and the dying for more than 50 years. Her selfless work among the poverty-stricken people of Kolkata is an inspiration for people all over the world and she was honoured with the Nobel Prize for Peace.

Mother Teresa

Jawaharlal Nehru, India's first Prime Minister, was educated in England. He was respected as a world statesman for his policies of peace, non-alignment and secularism. Nehru's most famous books are his 'Autobiography', 'Glimpses of World History' and 'Discovery of India'. Nehru loved children, and every year his birthday is celebrated as 'Children's Day'.

Mohan Das Karamchand Gandhi is the 'father of the nation'. While studying law in South Africa, he was disturbed by the oppression of Indians by the Whites. He formulated the path of Satyagraha and protested against the injustice. He returned to India and took up the leadership of the National Freedom struggle.

Mahatma Gandhi launched many movements to force the British out of India. The most well-known movements are the 'Non Cooperation Movement' (1920), 'Civil Disobedience Movement' (1930) and the 'Quit India Movement' (1942). In 1930, Gandhiji led the famous 'Dandi March' for breaking the Salt Laws. Gandhiji also worked hard for the upliftment of the 'harijans', the name given by him to the dalits. Gandhiji declared untouchability a sin against God and man.

Raja Ram Mohan Roy was a zealous social reformer with modern and progressive views. He stood firmly against all sort of social bigotry, conservatism and superstitions and advocated English and western education for his countrymen. A great scholar, he made a wide study of the different religions of the world, including Christianity and Islam. He also knew many languages like English, Persian, Arabic, Latin, French and Hebrew. He was also a great scholar of Bangla and translated the Vedas and Upanishads into Bengali.

He believed in the fundamental unity of all religions. He founded the 'Brahmo Samaj' to expose the religious hypocrisies and to check the growing influence of Christianity on Hindu society.

By far, the greatest achievement of Raja Ram Mohan Roy as a social reformer was the abolition of 'Sati' in 1829, child marriage and 'parda'.

Jawaharlal Nehru

Indira Gandhi

Subash Chandra Bose, popularly known as 'Netaji', was a great patriot and led the Indian National Army to fight for India's freedom. He gave to the nation the salutation and slogan of 'Jai Hind'. He was lost to the world in a plane crash in August 1945, but his death continues to be a mystery.

Subhash Chandra Bose

Indira Gandhi was the first woman Prime Minister of India. She was one of the most efficient Prime Ministers of India and is credited with the nationalisation of banks, liberation of Bangladesh and the 20-Point Programme for the upliftment of the poor. Mrs Gandhi met her tragic end on 31st October 1984, when she was assassinated by her own guards.

Kiran Bedi is a social activist and a retired Indian Police Service (IPS) officer. She became the first woman to join the IPS in 1972 and was last posted as Director General, Bureau of Police Research and Development, Ministry of Home Affairs. She was also the Inspector General of Police (Prisons) Tihar Jail, one of the world's largest prison complexes, and her prison reform policies led her to win the Ramon Magsaysay Award in 1994.

Kiran Bedi

Swami Vivekananda was a spiritual leader, yogi and patriot. In 1893, he went to Chicago as a representative of India at the Parliament of All Religions of the World. On 11th September, he delivered the historical speech which made his learned audience bow their heads in reverence. In 1897, he founded the Ramakrishna Mission for the service of the people.

Dr B R Ambedkar

Dr Bhim Rao Ambedkar was the main architect of the Indian Constitution. He was the inspiration behind the inclusion of a special provision in the Constitution of India for the development of the scheduled castes. Dr Ambedkar was the Law Minister of India from 1947 to 1951.

Dr. Ambedkar was the emancipator of the 'untouchables' and a crusader for social justice. This liberator of the downtrodden was affectionately called 'Baba Saheb'. He was posthumously awarded the Bharat Ratna in the year 1990.

Swami Vivekananda

Vallabhbhai Patel, often addressed as 'Sardar', was a political and social leader of India who played a major role in the country's struggle for independence and guided its integration into a united, independent nation. He led the Indian National Congress and was at the forefront of rebellions and political events.

Hailed as the 'Iron Man' of India, he is also remembered as the patron saint of India's civil servants for establishing the modern All-India Services.

Sri Aurobindo was an Indian nationalist and freedom fighter, poet, philosopher, and yogi. He joined the movement for India's freedom from British rule and became one of its most important leaders, before turning to developing his own vision and philosophy of human progress and spiritual evolution.

Sri Aurobindo

Vallabhbhai Patel

Vikram Sarabhai is considered the Father of the Indian Space Program. He played a leading role in the launching of India's first satellite, Aryabhata, in 1975.

Apart from being a scientist, he was a rare combination of an innovator, industrialist and visionary. He, along with other Ahmedabad-based industrialists played a major role in the creation of the Indian Institute of Management, Ahmedabad.

He was conferred the Padma Shri, and was posthumously awarded the Padma Vibushan in 1972.

The eminent scientist who ushered India into the atomic age was **Dr. Homi Jehangir Bhabha**.

It was largely due to his efforts that the nation's first Atomic research Center, now named Bhabha Atomic Research Centre, was established at Trombay, near Mumbai. In 1945, he founded the Tata Institute of Fundamental Research in Mumbai.

Jehangir Ratanji Dadabhoy Tata was a pioneer in Indian aviation. He was the first Indian pilot to qualify for a British private license. He founded Tata Airlines, which later came to be known as Indian Airlines. Tata was an early advocate of family planning, and he created the Family Planning Foundation in 1971. His innovations in India's fledgling hospitality and tourism industry as well as his contributions to scientific and technical research and corporate management gained public recognition from the Indian Government. He was honoured with the Bharat Ratna in 1991 and the United Nations Population Award in 1992.

Dhirubhai Ambani was an enterprising Indian entrepreneur. His life is reminiscent of the rags-to-riches story. He is remembered as the one who rewrote Indian corporate history and built a truly global corporate group.

He built Reliance Industries, India's largest private sector company. He created an equity cult in the Indian capital market. Reliance is the first Indian company to feature in the Forbes 500 list.

Ghanshyam Das Birla was a great architect of India's industrial growth. A multi-faceted personality, he laid the foundations of the Birla Empire and later founded the Federation of Indian Chambers of Commerce and Industry (FICCI), besides several educational institutions. He also established many temples, planetariums, and hospitals in his honour, the GD Birla Award for Scientific Research has been established to encourage scientists for their contribution in the various fields of scientific research.

Aditya Birla is the grandson of the legendary G D Birla, and was a successful business tycoon. His son, Kumarmangalam, is the present Chairman of the Birla group. He believed in expanding Indian businesses abroad and set up 19 companies outside India. This helped put the Birla group on the world map. He made the Birla Group, India's first multinational corporation.

C V Raman

C V Raman was a scientist in Physics, who won the Nobel Prize in 1930. His discovery of the 'Raman Effect' made a very distinctive contribution to Physics. He was knighted by the British Government in 1929. He was also conferred the title of Bharat Ratna in 1954.

Raman also conducted pioneering research in musical acoustics, particularly on the tamboura, the well-known Indian musical instrument.

Dr Homi Bhabha

Aditya Birla

41

Our Sports

Abhinav Bindra won the first individual Olympic gold medal for India in 2008.

Sachin Tendulkar was the first batsman in the world to complete 10,000 runs in ODI cricket.

Prakash Padukone was the first Indian to win the prestigious All England Badminton Championship in 1979. He also won the national senior title consecutively for nine years.

Kamlesh Mehta is till date the highest-ranked Indian table tennis player in Asian, Commonwealth and World ranking. He won the senior national title eight times.

Milkha Singh, 'The Flying Sikh' was the first Indian athlete to reach the Olympic finals of the 400 m at the 1960 Olympics. He finished 4th and missed the bronze medal by just a difference of 0.1 second!

Cricket

Since ancient times, physical culture has thrived in India. Early sports included weight lifting, archery, mace fighting, chariot racing, wrestling and races. The modern martial arts of the South-east are also said to have originated in India. India also lays claim to the birth of such games as chess and dice games like snakes and ladders. The popular games of today are of British introduction – cricket, hockey, football and tennis.

India's national game is **hockey**. The first hockey club was founded in the 1885-86 in Calcutta. This sport brought the first Olympic Gold to India in 1928. It was also the first Olympic gold medal won by Asia in the Olympics. India has won a total of eight gold medals in hockey at the Olympics. From the 1928 Amsterdam Olympics to the 1956 Melbourne Olympics India won six consecutive gold medals for hockey.

However, today India is known for its considerable **cricket** fan following. The India national cricket team won the 1983 Cricket World Cup and the 2007 ICC World Twenty20. The Indian team is currently ranked first by the ICC in Tests, and second in ODIs. The team has stalwarts like Virender Sehwag, who holds the record for the highest score (triple century) made by an Indian in Test cricket, which was also the fastest triple century in the history of international cricket. The Indian Premier League Twenty-Twenty contest took the cricketing world by storm and is a very popular contest in India.

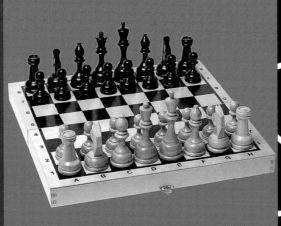

Chess

Football

In the indoor sports, Indians have won many laurels in the game of **chess**. Viswanathan Anand became the Grandmaster in 1988, when he was only 18! He is the current World Chess Champion. Koneru Humpy, all of 15 years old, became the youngest woman to be a grandmaster in 2002.

In other team sports, the first **football** game was organised in 1854 in Kolkata. In 1956, India became the first Asian nation to make it to the Olympic football semi-finals. India also won gold medals in the 1951 and 1962 Asian Games. Baichung Bhutia is the best known international face of Indian football.

Boxing is one of the lesser profiled sports in India. In 2007, India's M C Mary Kom won the best boxer title and also secured a hattrick of titles. During the 2008 Beijing Olympics, Vijender Kumar won a bronze medal in middleweight boxing while Akhil Kumar, Jitender Kumar, A L Lakra and Dinesh Kumar each won a bronze medal. Vijender Kumar is current world number 1 in middleweight boxing.

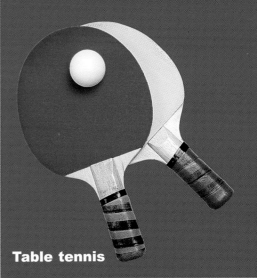

Table tennis

Golf is an emerging sport in India. The most successful Indian golfer is Jeev Milkha Singh who has won titles all over the world, namely three during the European Tour, four during the Japan Golf Tour and six during the Asian Tour. Other Indians who have won the Asian tour order of merit are Jyoti Randhawa in 2002 (the first Indian to achieve this) and Arjun Atwal.

Golf

Tennis is popular among Indians in urban areas. Leander Paes and Mahesh Bhupathi have won many Men's Doubles and Mixed Doubles Grand Slam Titles. Sania Mirza is the only notable Indian woman tennis player having won the WTA title and breaking in to the Top 30 WTA ranking. Yuki Bhambri and Somdev Devvarman are Yuki is the current Australian Open Junior Singles champion.

Education and Modernisation

In ancient times before the development of letters, knowledge was transmitted orally from generation to generation. After the development of letters, the oral literature was put down on palm leaves and the barks of trees and education spread further. Temples and monasteries became centres of education.

The *guru-shishya* tradition is said to be the most ancient style of education in India. Herein the student (*shishya*) was supposed to stay in the house/hermitage of the guru and learn from him. These institutions were not run for monetary purposes but there was a tradition of the student making an offering or being asked to do something special when he left. This was known as *Guru dakshina*.

"*The real difficulty is that people have no idea of what education truly is. We assess the value of education in the same manner as we assess the value of land or of shares in the stock-exchange market. We want to provide only such education as would enable the student to earn more. We hardly give any thought to the improvement of the character of the educated. The girls, we say, do not have to earn; so why should they be educated? As long as such ideas persist there is no hope of our ever knowing the true value of education.*"

Mahatma Gandhi

With the spread of Buddhism, education spread more widely and this led to the establishment of some world famous educational institutions at Nalanda, Vikramshila and Takshashila. These institutes arose from monasteries. Nalanda University in Bihar flourished from the 5th to 13th century AD, with about 10,000 resident students and teachers on its roll at one time.

In the medieval period, *Agraharas* were spread across southern India. Roughly translated, *agraharas* were ancient-day boarding schools imparting primary education. Talagunda or Sthanakundur appears to have been the earliest *agrahara* in medieval Karnataka. Royal patronage by able kings also supported the cause of education. It was required of boys to learn different languages, which enabled them to travel from one region to another, for reasons of trade, pilgrimage and learning.

The Muslim children were educated in madrassas. These institutions were originally established to spread the message of Islam and impart religious teaching to its faithful followers. The Ulamas or religious specialists were the teachers. These educational institutions also imparted higher education at one time. Muslims established elementary and secondary schools in the 11th century.

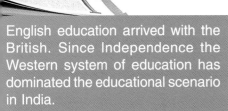

The government had established the University Grants Commission (UGC) to develop the higher education system. The UGC's main role has been to regulate the standard and spread of higher education in India. Today India has more than 17000 colleges, 20 central universities, 217 State Universities, 106 Deemed Universities and 13 institutes of National importance. There are also numerous private institutes in India that offer various professional courses.

The institutes of higher education that are internationally renowned include the group of fifteen autonomous engineering and technology-oriented institutes known as the Indian Institutes of Technology (IITs), declared as Institutes of National Importance by the Parliament of India. The Indian Institutes of Management (IIMs) are the top graduate business schools in India set up by the government. All seven are completely autonomous institutes owned and financed by the Central Government of India. Established in 1956, the All India Institute of Medical Sciences (AIIMS) is a premier medical education institute that offers undergraduate and postgraduate courses in medicine.

The fields of study have diversified considerably. Today's generation can apply for courses in fashion and designing in premier institutes like the National Institute of Fashion Technology (NIFT) and National Institute of Design (NID). They may opt for courses in law, filmmaking, photography, aviation, theatre, music and dance. The opportunities are endless and the horizon wide open.

India is the second largest provider of scientists and IT experts in the world today, putting the Indian IT industry at par with the Silicon Valley.

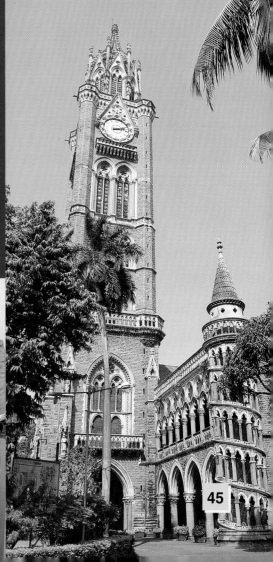

English education arrived with the British. Since Independence the Western system of education has dominated the educational scenario in India.

In India, elementary education means eight years of schooling from the age of six. The 86th constitutional amendment has made elementary education a fundamental right for children. Despite that, the total literacy rate in India is 65.38%.